T0064510

Babies Come From Where?!

Amber Owens

BALBOA.
PRESS

A DIVISION OF HAY HOUSE

Balboa Press books may be ordered through booksellers or by contacting:

Balboa Press
A Division of Hay House
1663 Liberty Drive
Bloomington, IN 47403
www.balboapress.com
1 (877) 407-4847

Because of the dynamic nature of the Internet, any web addresses or
links contained in this book may have changed since publication and
may no longer be valid. The views expressed in this work are solely those
of the author and do not necessarily reflect the views of the publisher,
and the publisher hereby disclaims any responsibility for them.

The author of this book does not dispense medical advice or prescribe the use
of any technique as a form of treatment for physical, emotional, or medical
problems without the advice of a physician, either directly or indirectly. The
intent of the author is only to offer information of a general nature to help
you in your quest for emotional and spiritual well-being. In the event you use
any of the information in this book for yourself, which is your constitutional
right, the author and the publisher assume no responsibility for your actions.

Any people depicted in stock imagery provided by Thinkstock are
models, and such images are being used for illustrative purposes only.
Certain stock imagery © Thinkstock.

Print information available on the last page.

ISBN: 978-1-5043-3950-6 (sc)
ISBN: 978-1-5043-3951-3 (e)

Library of Congress Control Number: 2015913786

Balboa Press rev. date: 09/02/2015

Chord 1

Lullaby Lake

B ina sits Indian-style on the park bench near the edge of the lake. She feels the sunshine kissing her skin while she observes the creation all around her. She watches the shimmering crystal-like water freely flowing in front of her, and meditates on what it means to feel free and at peace and in love. She looks down at her baby son, Cadence, who sits comfortably in her lap. Comfortable, yet hot. Little beads of sweat appear on Cadence's hairline.

Bina wipes his sweat away with her hand, then kisses his temple. She gets a whiff of baby scent coming from his head. Even the hint of his infant musk smells irresistibly sweet to her; intoxicating, actually. She sniffs his sweaty head repeatedly, thankful to be a mom with the ability to have such access to this innocent little being. Grateful that she is allowed to love with such intensity.

Only a mother's love causes a woman to inhale the funk of little toes that have been stuffed in socks all day. Or of tiny fingers that are somewhat stinky from dried drool. Or of precious ears that have trapped dirt in the miniscule crevices. Or the barely- there neck that is tart from old milk, which has secretly nestled in the rolls under the chin. She breathes in love from his cherished body. This fragile morsel of goodness and joy set before her has captured her heart completely.

Peeking down, she catches him staring studiously at her, finding her absolutely more fascinating than the natural world around them. He studies her with such alertness and curiosity, as if memorizing every freckle and hair on her face. His big, bright gray tinted eyes travel from Bina's long, wavy hair, to her forehead, nose and lips, then back to her eyes. She sees her reflection in his eyes so clearly, like a mirror. Except her reflection in his eyes is more radiant than in any mirror; unblemished and perfectly defined. Only she exists in his eyes.

Their loving gaze instills calmness, and brings a smile on both of their faces. He gently touches her lips with his teeny right hand. The softness of his tiny fingers makes her nibble on them. He chuckles, revealing the dimples in his cheeks. She treasures moments like this, knowing they will pass too fast.

He pushes his lips up and out for a kiss, to which she gladly gives, almost wanting to bite him because he's so deliciously cute. She feels inspired to sing a verse from "Sun Is Shining," one of her favorites by Bob Marley:

> "Sun is shining.
> Weather is sweet, yeah.
> Makes you wanna move
> Your dancing feet.
> To the rescue,
> Here I am."

She knows he loves it when she sings to him, especially when she's holding him tight.

Deeply fixed on her eyes, he attentively soaks in her melody. He still rests his little fingers on her bottom lip, opening his mouth as if tasting her words. At that moment, birds from afar cast shadows over Bina and baby Cadence, flickering their wings against the blue sky backdrop.

"Look, Peanut, at the birds flying up and down and in and out; they're dancing in the air. And see there," Bina points to the trees that dance to the silent beat of the silky wind, and Cadence's head turns accordingly to follow her instructions.

"Even the trees move to the rhythm of the breeze. All of nature dances together; and if we take a moment to enjoy it, we also have the ability to sway with everything in our own human way. Listen closely, and you'll hear the music."

She makes sure to speak to Cadence with a level of respect, not with a patronizing *baby voice*. Although Cadence usually soaks in her intellectual conversations with ease, this time he gives her an awkward gaze, wrinkling his eyebrows together at her. His head tilts slightly as if to ask, "Music – what music are you speaking of?"

She notices his intrigued expression, "What's wrong baby? You don't like music? But you like when I sing to you."

A huge grin reveals his toothless gums and unsullied pink tongue.

"Ah ha, got'cha! You like my songs, don't you babe?" she emphasizes while tickling his underarm. "And so does the *tickle monster*! Grrr!" Whenever she tickles him, she makes sure to introduce the "tickle monster."

He squirms and giggles uncontrollably, compressing his arm into his side with all his strength, obviously hoping it will prevent her from continuing the task. He closes his eyes, and laughs until he can't breath. He wheezes a little while catching his breath. He opens his eyes when she stops tickling, and makes a cute little squeal.

Bina thinks to herself: If he could talk, I bet he'd say, "Goodie! Now that my eyes are open, I can see that it's **you**, and not that *tickle monster* creep who was just here." She laughs at the idea of him talking. Oh, the things he would say! She can only imagine.

"Son, do you know how much I love you? Too much to describe with words! And I know that you love me just as much, with all of your little heart. Someone asked me how I know that you actually love me, and don't just think I'm the 'food truck'. I replied that love isn't simply a thought or emotion. It's an electric connection. When it's there, we just 'know' – without thinking about it or even *feeling* it."

Cadence seems to enjoy her keen enthusiasm regarding her concept of love because he belts out a "teehee" and claps his hands.

Bina kisses his nose, "You agree, eh? That's why I like talking to you because you get me. Hey, that concept about love is kind-of profound, right?"

Bina whips out a small journal from her purse (which is also the diaper bag), and begins writing. She writes a complex version of what she just said about love. Cadence inspects the paper like he can read. He leans over, pressing his weight onto Bina's thigh, towards the paper she writes on. His neck stretches out and his perfectly rounded head bobbles slightly from his shift forward. His eyes are wide with vigilance, intently fixed on her paper.

Unexpectedly, Bina hears a man's blood-curdling voice whisper, "What are you writing?"

She jumps from startled nerves. Her skin prickles with goosebumps. She looks up expecting to see someone standing there, but sees nobody. Cadence's small body jolts slightly from her frightened movement. He practically drops out of her lap onto the ground, but she recovers her secure hold on him.

The spooky voice continues at her, "Why make the easiest things so complex?"

The raspy whisper is so close, it sounds like someone speaking into her ear. But nobody else is around except herself and Cadence.

She crouches down placing her nose on the infant's head, "That was weird. Did you hear that, Cadence?" she asks, simultaneously pulling his body closer to hers.

Cadence looks back at her, raising his eyes up, and replies in a diabolic tone, "Of course I heard, after all *I* asked it."

Pause. Silence. Bina is frozen. She just looks at her baby, a wee-bit too frightened to get up and run.

Cadence clears his throat, "Excuse the raspy voice. Sorry bout that. Whoa, I must have sounded so scary! AhhhHaaaHaaa!" He laughs to himself placing his hands on his little belly. "I should've cleared my throat a long time ago. But I hesitated because I love that clogged feeling that makes my voice sound deep and gruff. You know what I mean?"

Bina keeps in silent astonishment, staring at the talking infant.

He continues, "Anyhoo. I think it's time I tell you, only because I love you, that you tend to ramble on about things. Your thoughts are so beautiful when you express them simply. But when you write, you drown them in words."

She finally breaks the locked stare to examine her surroundings. She first looks left, then right, then behind. She hopes that this is some kind of not-so-funny joke. "Ok, which internet prank show am I on?"

Confused, he asks while tapping her knee, "Prank show? Bina, it's *really me*. Are you going crazy or something?"

Her heart pounds so fast that she feels it will pop out at any second. Tempted to toss the baby into the lake and flee for her life, Bina remains seated. She regains her composure, but now *her* eyes are wide as she studies Cadence's face in wonderment. Stillness. He sits smiling up at her sensing her tension.

"Ok, so don't freak out," Cadence suggests, putting his miniature palms up in the air.

"Too late, I already am. My baby is talking clearly, and in a foreign accent. Why would I not freak out? Of course I'm freaking out! A baby, MY baby, is talking, with a grown man's voice, in a foreign accent. And I'm responding... to my baby... who speaks like a man." Bina's shoulders tensely raise higher and higher as she speaks from the awkwardness of the situation.

"Actually, I'm not *your* baby. Well, I mean, yes, 'technically' I'm your baby, but 'literally' I'm not your baby." Then he quickly interrupts himself and waves his hands near her face, shaking his head, "But Bina, listen, Bina, listen: that's not why I'm telling you don't freak out. An extremely large bird is headed our way, and I know you're terrified of birds... "

Before he can finish his statement, she interrupts with a loud gasp and shuts her eyes. As if her five month old talking baby isn't crazy enough. Let alone, her talking baby who is telling her that he's actually not even her baby. And now she's learning that a super-duper gigantic bird is hurling at her from the sky, her worst nightmare! What is happening?

Bina opens her eyes, covering her head. She catches a glimpse of what she thinks is a stork crashing into the lake. The splash from its fall creates a petite tidal wave reaching Bina and Cadence with a heavy sprinkle. From what she saw before the plunge, this isn't any ordinary stork. It definitely has the overall appearance of a stork – long sword-like beak, white feathers, and lanky legs.

But the wingspan looked much larger than that of any stork. And the body is as plump as that of an ostrich. The thing is huge! Bina has never seen such attributes on a stork before. Despite her increasing intimidation of the majestic mammoth of a bird, Bina is curious to see it soon safely eject from the lake.

"Did you see if the stork had a very large blanket in its beak?" Cadence anxiously asks her.

"Ummm, I think so. It looked like a gold blanket. I only caught a glimpse." Bina assumes it was gold from how it sparkled in the sunset.

Still skeptical, Bina watches for the stork to emerge and the package it had with it. The whole while, Cadence observes, not the fallen bird, but Bina's reaction to it all.

Finally, a white feathered tip appears from the water creating a small wave. Then the whole creature rises out, flapping its wings, splashing frantically, and gasping for air. Its ample, drenched body flies up from the lake to the edge of the grass. It hovers over them like a daunting giant. Its reddish-orange legs are thick like small tree trunks. Its body topped with a shiny black head. And its black and white wings have muscles under the multitude of feathers like a bodybuilder's arms.

It plops down directly in front of Bina and Cadence, displaying its true enormity! It places its bulky wings on its shins (since his knees bend backwards behind his body), and gurgles out the excess water from its chiseled red beak.

Bina quickly kicks her legs out at the stork, and leans down hiding her face behind Cadence's mini body.

"Oh, that's good – hide behind the baby. *He'll* protect you from a nine foot, 200 pound bird," the stork snarls at Bina.

At this point, Bina finds it fitting to scream. She yelps, fiercely warning the bird to keep away.

Cadence twists at his waist to lean back and put his hands on each of Bina's cheeks. Gently lifting her head up, cupping her face, he says, "Don't be afraid. The bird is right: I *can* protect you," and smiles at her.

Amidst all this craziness of whoever (or whatever) Cadence is, his smile is still the most calming thing she's ever seen. The power of his smile puts her at ease.

Cadence turns back around to the stork, who is shaking out droplets of water from its peculiarly large semi-webbed, semi-clawed feet, and is muttering, "I don't get paid enough for this."

Cadence stands up confidently on his stubby legs, points his pudgy index finger at the stork, and asks, "Scott, really?! Why would you upset the lady like that? Didn't your mother teach you that you gotta be gentle with the ladies? And what's up with that so-called landing you just did?"

Scott hiccups a few times.

"Awe man, those hiccups tell me you've been over-eating again. Haven't you? You know doing that gives you a sleepy high. You're supposed to fly, not *fly*."

"Are you accusing me of flying off a food high? That's total animal cruelty," Scott rants. "Don't blame me for the crash. You need to talk to your little girlfriend about that, not me."

Bina cannot believe that she's still sitting there experiencing this. She wonders who Scott is referring to as Cadence's girlfriend.

"Girlfriend? Me? Pssh, I don't think so. Nobody can tie me down. I'm what's called a *play-ya*."

"Cadence, you don't even know what either a girlfriend or being a player means. You just hear the adults use those terms, and think it sounds cool. Am I right?"

"Well... you don't know everything, Scott!" Cadence puts his hand on the side of his mouth to cover his words from Bina. He wiggles his fingers as he speaks in a secretive tone, "Stop embarrassing me in front of Bina! She thinks I'm mysterious and cool."

Their banter begins to sound like background noise to Bina. She is too distracted by the waves in the lake behind the stork, which are gradually rippling from underneath the surface.

Instantly - Poof! The gold blanket pops up from the center of the ripples. It rests on the lake, bobbing along, gliding towards Bina and the others as if being hauled in by an invisible boat. It arrives swiftly to the edge of the lake in front of Bina and the others. Cadence and Scott don't notice amidst their arguing.

"Um, excuse me, Cadence. The bird's gold blanket just floated to the shore," Bina nods her head in the direction of the sack. Cadence and Scott stop and focus their attention on the gold blanket.

Punches from the inside of the sack knock once, then twice, then three times, before the blanket springs up onto the grass. Gold dust specks trickle around it as it thumps down, making a drum beat sound upon landing. Enchanting music sounds out from nowhere.

Cadence applauds, and jumps off of Bina's lap to meet the bundle. He begins unraveling it carefully, humming a happy tune under his breath. Each unfolded piece of the blanket falls into a gold dust pile and blows into the breeze. The fire flies now appearing as night comes, illuminate the gold specks blowing into the air.

Finally, Cadence steps to the side so that Bina has a clear view of the unveiling. "Bina, this is Cavatina," Cadence introduces with one little hand stretched out.

An angelic baby girl is bashfully curled up in a ball. She raises her head, and places attention on Bina. She accentuates her steel blue eyes by innocently batting her long, curly lashes. Her butterball face and puckered pink lips melt Bina's heart. They all become mesmerized watching Cavatina stretch up out of the fetal position onto her pudgy feet.

Then, unanticipatedly, a spotlight shines on her. The enchanting music shifts from a smooth and satiny melody, to a flavorful flow of drum beats, up-tempo piano notes and guitar bass booms. The tune sounds like a contemporary hip-hop version of Beethoven's "5th Symphony". Cadence claps in rhythm to the beat as Cavatina begins to groove.

Cavatina's oval eyes peer straight ahead at the small crowd in front of her. Her rosy cheeks curve at the top from the somewhat rugged smirk on her face. She strides closer to them, synchronizing each tubby foot to step one zig- zag in front of the other, perfectly to the beat. Her body bounces like an adorable, squishy little ball. When she arrives just inches away from Bina, she jiggles her booty down into a squat position, while simultaneously bobbing her shoulders.

She then swings her elbows out in the air like little chunky chicken wings. She wiggles her body around in a 360 degree twirl. Then finally she jumps into the air and back down in slow motion like a rock star.

The music stops, and the spotlight dissolves away. Cavatina stands proudly, with her pudgy arms raised straight up as if she just successfully completed a gymnastics routine. Her chest puffs noticeably up and down with dramatic, heavy breath. Catching her breath with a triumphant smile, "I made it," she says.

Cadence applauds the performance, "Stimu, stimu, Cavatina!" Nudging Bina to join in, "Isn't she fun, Bina?"

Bina gives Cadence a half-way nod of agreement, unsure of what "stimu" means. She asks him, "*Stimu?* What does that mean?"

"Oh, that's just a clever little dilly I made up." He proudly pretends to brush invisible dirt off his shoulder. "Took it from the first part of the word *stimulating*. I say it when something is stimulatingly awesome. Can't use it if something is just mediocre. Only awesome," he clarifies.

Scott yawns loudly to imply that he's not impressed. "I'm sorry. Did I interrupt the yakkety yak? Please continue. This is **so** entertaining. Not trivial at all."

Cavatina begins to explain why she dropped in, "Word in the sky is that you picked an adult to tour through the hood – babyhood, that is."

Scott sarcastically runs off at the mouth, "Oh, I see what you just did there: you tried to use hip-lingo to make yourself seem cool."

She puts her hand up. If Scott were shorter, it would be in his face.

"So as I was saying! Scott and I changed route to get here immediately because I wanna tag along with you. Ya know, since I'm your fun half." Cavatina winks at Cadence, and leans against him.

"Ha! You wish you were my fun half," Cadence wittingly remarks. "But you're right, the tour is never as fun unless you're with me."

The babies enthusiastically high-5 each other.

"Well then, now that you're here, let's get this party started," he initiates.

They commence to shooing Scott away so they can get started with Bina's tour of babyhood. Cadence flags his hand at Scott and in a nasalized voice urges, "Shoo-shoo. Skedaddle kid, you bother me!"

Cavatina and Bina both laugh at Cadence's attempt at a 1940's movie star gangster accent; as well as the equally entertaining look of mortification on Scott's face from being commanded to shoo away.

"Well, I've never felt so insulted in my life. Fine then, I know when I'm not needed anymore," Scott gripes, preparing for flight by adjusting his posture. Shaking his elongated beak from left to right, he stretches his towering body. Exposing his tremendously lengthy wingspan, he reminds Bina of why she felt cowardly when first meeting him.

"I'll see you two in a bit, after you're done with your excursions and are ready to finally do some *actual* work," Scott sarcastically remarks.

"And as for *you*..." swiftly pointing his sharp-edged beak and beady eyes at Bina, causing her head to jerk back in alarm. Scott growls, "...We'll never meet again. But now you'll think of me every time a stork lands. The babies will explain the details, and you'll be grateful for us storks instead of fearful. Oh yea, and on that note: you really don't have to fear birds. But I guess you'll learn that in another story, on another day.

"Congratulations on your honor of being chosen to journey through babyhood. It will answer the long- asked query of where babies come from... and it surely is not the gruesome story that adults have passed on for generations! Just nasty if you ask me!" He tucks his long neck inward and begins flapping his wings.

Bina watches Scott soar away until he finally fades unrecognizably into the night clouds. Cadence and Cavatina begin to talk to each other in hand signs and random facial expressions.

When Cadence realizes Bina is analyzing them, he explains what they're doing. "We're just deciding who will tell you which parts of the story. I want all the fun stuff, and Cavatina can take all the tid-bits."

"Hey," Cavatina whines, "*I* wanted to tell most of the story. You should do the short parts."

"Noooo!" Cadence shakes his head briskly. Still showing a smile, he argues, "No, she's MY adult, and I should be the one to tell her most of it."

Cavatina looks at the ground in defeat, and mumbles, "Okay."

At first, Cadence pumps his palms in 'raise the roof' motion, celebrating his victory. But not wanting Cavatina feeling too bad that she lost the argument, he affectionately suggests, "Well, how about we play the 'you see, we see' game? That way it's equally fun for both of us. And just so you're not sad, I'll even let you blow the travel bubble."

Cavatina excitedly balls her fist and shakes them in front of her chubby face. "Really? You'll let me blow the travel bubble? Yippee! You're the best, Cadence!" She then does a shimmy with her shoulders and adds jazz hands to it.

"But not the nose bubble! Only the mouth bubble, k, Cavatina?!"

"Awe man! Nose bubbles are my favorite. That's ok. I'm still happy! Give me one little minute."

She steps back and begins a bubbling noise by vibrating her lips like a sail boat engine. Bubbles trickle from her lips, until one jumbo bubble begins to float along side her.

"While Cavatina is perfecting the travel bubble, let me give you a heads-up on a few things. First, what's gonna happen is that you'll reminisce on what **you see** as an adult parent. Then **we'll** reveal to you what's *really* happening from a baby's point of view. That's why the game is called 'you see, we see.' Feel free to stop us at any time with questions.

"Second, there's a reason why adults don't remember babyhood. It's because they were never actually babies at all. Cavatina and I are the only two babies in existence who travel to adults. Large storks, like Scott, deliver us at a speed faster than light or any other medium known to adults. It's the speed of music. We are not contained in single physical bodies, which explains how we can exist with different families in different forms at one time.

"This is also why all babies look alike at first because we are literally the same: myself for boys, and Cavatina for girls. What we eventually morph into is a gradual reflection of the adults we are assigned to. Usually, we'll take on the form of the adult with the more dominant personality, or whoever other adults say we're starting to look like. The point is, our physical appearance is really only in the adult mind. Even in this moment, the voice you hear is just in your imagination; what you imagine my voice as."

Bina thinks to herself, "I imagine Cadence with a grown man's voice? How unconventional." But before they can elaborate on the topic, Cavatina's voice rings out,

"Alright guys, it's ready."

"Stimu!" Cadence emphatically shouts out.

"Hop in!" Cavatina instructs, and enters the travel bubble first.

Bina looks down at Cadence, who smiles re-assuredly at her. His perfect smile warms her heart with love and happiness. She steps into the bubble with Cavatina, and Cadence follows after her.

"So this is why babies make the drool bubbles, huh? Wow, and all this time adults thought 'raspberries' were associated with teething. But really every time babies blow bubbles, they're preparing to travel through the story of babyhood with an adult. How interesting."

The babies chuckle at Bina's naivety.

"Bina, Bina, Bina. You're so silly! Always making something more complicated than it is," Cadence says with his fluffy hand on his forehead, shaking his head. "We just want to take you in the bubble while we explain cuz' it's **fun**."

Bina's cheeks become flushed from the slight embarrassment of her assumptions, "Oh."

Cadence and Cavatina innocently giggle again, which helps remind Bina not to take herself so seriously. And so she joins in the giggling.

The blimp sized bubble lifts the three off the ground into the sky. Cadence sits down and pats the empty space next to him, motioning for Bina to sit there. She feels the flow of music speed, where there is practically no time at all because it's so fast. The sky is nothing like Bina always thought it to be. She beholds various colors everywhere. It's not dark, neither are there cottony clouds everywhere. And there is no beginning and no end, no earth or sky boundaries.

"Space only looks dark and divided to adults because they have closed off their imaginations beyond their own realm. They feel infinity is impossible. But everything dances together in the universe without limits. This is a major part of our mission as babies, to help adults remember that," Cadence says out loud as if he knows what Bina was just thinking.

Chord 2

Musical Universe

C olors that Bina has never seen surround them. Some flash by, some bounce, others dissipate into mist. Others feel hot, cold or other sensations she never knew existed. Palpable colors.

Not only that, but each color emits an emotion. New emotions that she's experiencing for the first time. She can't describe in words what she feels because everything is new and unknown and miraculous. Words aren't needed, only the feeling is important right now.

She closes her eyes, tilts her head back, and breathes in deeply, then out slowly. The melodious sounds of violins and piano fill the air. She soaks in the savory moment without restraint, and can't help but smile.

Resounding colors that encircle the travel bubble help Bina understand what the universe is. It's just what Cadence had mentioned and more: it's colorful music, a harmonious blend of love and life. It is not what adults classify as music, though. This music is more than just simple sounds and rhythmic patterns. It transcends any imagined separations within the universe, so that even someone without sound sensory or touch would be able to experience these positive vibrations.

"That's what each day feels like as a baby," Cavatina's tiny voice says.

Bina happily anticipates this surreal adventure. Both Cadence and Cavatina are such precious, harmless babies with great secrets of knowledge to share. Who could dare leave their pure innocence? Who wouldn't want to experience the awe-inspiring joy of these amazing little beings? Who would neglect listening to the message they so kindly want to deliver to adults? Not Bina.

Bina isn't running because her love and obligation as a mother is too strong to abandon her baby, no matter who or what he is. Although she's uncertain about this scenario, she sees this opportunity to understand her baby better. And, in turn, get a better sense of being a parent – a mom. Sure this moment is far from the usual, and nothing Bina ever expected, but she is grateful for this mystical journey. Perhaps her unwavering love accounts for why she is one of the few chosen to learn where babies truly come from.

"We've mastered a melody for each adult who appears on earth," Cadence explains.

The way Cadence says *appears on earth* prompts Bina to ask,

"Well, how **do** adults *appear on earth* if we were never babies?" She anticipates some grand revelation of where adults come from in the answer Cadence will give.

"How do we know? We're just babies," he replies. "All we know about adults is what directly pertains to us in our mission."

Cavatina diverts the conversation to her. Like a little doll, she cutely puts her hands under her double chin and locks her fingers together,

"Getting back to us being the only two babies who travel to adults: I'm obviously the faster one at mastering the music because there are more girl babies than boy babies delivered to adults."

"Yea, so! You might be a little, teensy-weensy bit faster. But I think I'm the true master here because boys are waaaaaay more in demand. Guess it goes to show that you can't rush perfection. Perfection takes its sweet time!"

Cadence lifts his shoulders confidently, glancing at Bina for attention.

Bina gushes over how adorable they both are.

Cavatina shakes her head and sips air through her gums, "But girls are always cuter and more snugly, so I'm pretty sure we're the better package."

"Go ahead and believe what you'd like, my little female friend. But nobody stinks better than boys can stink. I reek of goodness. You ain't got nothing on my cuteness!"

"Ewe! Why do you think that **stink** equals **cute**? That doesn't even make sense. And what do you mean by: *female friend* ?" Cavatina apparently takes that as an insult.

"Exactly! You're proving my point. If you don't even know that adults love smelling babies, stinky or not, then you don't know the basics of baby cuteness! And yea, aren't you my *female friend*?"

"Sure I am... I'm your *female* friend, who happens to work harder than you do, and kicks your butt at finishing missions!"

"Aaaaahhhh, haaaa-haaaa! Now *that* is laughable, mate. Forget being a baby, forget being a female friend. You need to be a comedian with the jokes you have!"

Cadence returns to his explanation, "Anyhoo, Bina, now that you know the basics, it's a perfect time to start the you-see-we-see game. So let your mind flashback throughout your experience with me as your baby."

He gives himself a hug, to show Bina that he knows he's cute, his little arms barely able to stretch across his chest.

"The music will guide you. Don't just tell the story, but really imagine the adventure as you see it, from your heart. The colors will play the melody of your thoughts and emote it for us. From there, we will play a melody back so that you know what *we* saw happening at that same moment. 3-2-1 let's go." Cadence gestures at Bina in an Elvis Presley pose.

Bina chuckles, and rhetorically asks, "Ok, so I just close my eyes, and let my thoughts run free?"

Closing her eyes, she pays close attention to the acoustic guitar that starts playing in her ears, feeling warmth from the nearest passing color.

Chord 3

In The Beginning

Bina sits in the hospital bed, reflecting on the past nine months of excitement. Aside from the constant dizzy spells, nausea, weight gain, water retention, mood swings, and other unmentionables, these recent months have been the most wonderful of her whole life. Every day brought something new, pushing her one day closer to meeting the best little person in the whole wide world. Nothing else has mattered except staying healthy in order to nurture the awesome human growing inside of her womb, and nothing else would ever compare again. Waking up each morning, never alone, always full of love. Despite the haste of wanting the precious joy cuddled in her arms, she didn't ever want these moments to end of the baby safe inside her belly.

It's time! Bina awaits, not knowing what to expect. Pressure, pains, hours pass. She hears the doctor congratulate her on her healthy baby boy.

"Does he look like a Cadence, babe?" she asks the baby's father, faint of breath. She hears him answer,

"Yes, he's definitely a Cadence. Not sure who he looks like yet, but he's our boy!"

She looks up to see the most beautiful creature being carried over to the bed and placed on her chest. Little Cadence. He's so fragile. He's so tiny. He's so happy to be with Bina, looking up with giant gray colored eyes and pale skin which hasn't retained color yet.

The hand- knitted cap covers his entire head, practically covering his face, protecting him from the cool hospital draft. Seeing his limbs all tucked into the blanket makes Bina anxious to take them out and analyze each little toe and finger. But she's too enamored, and exhausted, to do anything except stare and say, "Cadence, I love you so much already!" She sighs with tears rolling down her cheeks, "I love you," she echoes and presses her dry lips onto his tiny cheek.

"Notice the fontanel, at the top of the head, is still very soft, and will remain so until early toddler years. So take caution to be gentle, but not paranoid because babies are more resilient than you think. On occasion, it may pulsate. There's no definite explanation for this but it seems it may happen when the baby is becoming dehydrated," the doctor explains to Bina. "And the red marks between his eyes, on his eyelids, around his nostrils, under his nose, and behind his neck are nothing to worry about. They'll go away within a couple years." Bina is curious as to what they are.

The doctor defines, "Oh, we don't have a definite explanation for the cause of these marks either. Some babies are just randomly born with them. They're what we have nicknamed in the medical field as 'stork bites.' Nothing to worry about. As I mentioned, it just happens to some babies as a temporary birth mark. The most important thing is that this little bundle of joy is healthy. Just enjoy this time while you can. He'll be grown before you know it, having his own children."

The words resonate in her head, causing a little anxiety at the thought of Cadence one day leaving her arms. But deep down inside, she knows that Cadence will always be her baby, no matter how old he gets. As the doctor speaks, she catches a glimpse of Cadence, who tries hard to zoom in on her face, but instead goes cross-eyed attempting to focus. One of his little hands finds its way out of the blanket and clenches her finger, bracing on for dear life. She is his everything, all that he knows and trusts. And she's ok with that because he's all that's real to her, all that's worth living for.

We See...

Cadence receives "Assignment – Bina" as his next mission. Floating through time in a travel bubble, he reviews a full description of Bina: a beautiful composition. It's comprised of Bina's lifestyle and personality reading. It flows with peaceful rhythm, soothing and organized, meticulously loving. He has a feeling she will be a chosen one, just from the rhythm of her composition.

He immediately begins to implant the connector program, which is a special chemical structure. He inserts the program into her brain and heart by humming a tune at the universe. This program will prepare her physically, emotionally and mentally for the coming baby. Preparing her for activities such as holding and carrying him constantly, responding patiently to his cry, endlessly picking up objects he repeatedly throws, properly reacting to his silly faces, and so on.

As Cadence implants the connector program into Bina's body, he observes her reaction. Although the process only takes less than seconds for Cadence, the experience lasts nine months for Bina in adult time.

He comments to the universe while observing Bina, "It never ceases to amaze me, watching the adult body's reaction to the connector chemicals. Their hearts expand with so much love that their bellies swell, making room for all the joy. After all, love comes from the heart, joy comes from the gut. Then they somehow absorb all the love, transferring strength throughout their entire bodies, until their hearts and bellies eventually deflate to their original sizes. It's amazing!

"Interesting, too, they think **we** actually grow inside of and exit out of *their bodies*. Really?! That would *kill* them! Funny little adults with their crazy antics."

He watches Bina with keen interest. She exhibits all kinds of freakish symptoms, like the majority of adults do, while connecting with the purity of babies.

Finally, Cadence has reached the meeting station, waiting for his flight. "Scott, buddy," he joyfully greets the stork as it lands with an empty gold blanket in its beak. "I haven't seen you for the last few assignments. Had to use the other storks. You took a vacation, eh?"

"Enough of the small talk." Scott cuts him off. "Let's just be quick, like in Cavatina's missions. She's actually very brilliant in her efficiency. You should take a lesson or two from the girl."

Cadence rolls his eyes, "It's ok, no thanks. I'd rather be cute than quick. Know what I mean? Heeheehee!" he puts out his hand for a high-five.

Scott raises one eyebrow, unamused, not moving or saying anything in reply. Aware of Scott's annoyance, Cadence clears his throat,

"Anyhoo, Hospital Route 77 please. Assignment Bina."

"Yep, I got the memo. No need for you to reiterate," Scott replies in his usual sarcastic tone as he bends low to Cadence's eye level.

"Haaahaaa, I don't know what I'd do without your dry humor to start my assignments, Scott." He taps Scott's head before hopping into the gold blanket hanging on Scott's beak. He ties a secure knot closing himself inside the sack.

During the flight, he practices his cry, excited to soon display his vocals for the first time to Bina. He also finishes the last of the connector program, implanting the memories of labor and delivery by humming a tune. "I always procrastinate on this part," he reveals out loud sounding muffled from inside the sack, "because I dread having to design the memories of what seems like such trauma. One thing I never include in the memory is any final pain. Adults *want* to remember pain, for some odd reason. But if they really experienced the pain they *think* they did, then they wouldn't want to keep having us babies!"

Out of nowhere, turbulence strikes, bopping Cadence around violently inside the bundle. "Whoa, whoa, whoa! What's happening, Scott?"

"No worries, I'm awake, I'm awake!"

"Scott, you were falling asleep? Are you insane, man? Now we're seconds off track, or to the adults, hours off track. Drats, I have to hurry and formulate a detour memory!"

Cadence scrambles to think up a program which will account for the delay of his arrival in Bina's memory. He sings the melody hastily so it implants into Bina's mind in a flash. While this is happening, more turbulence rumbles, causing a piece of the blanket to open up just enough for Cadence's head to begin slipping out.

Bloop! He sees blue sky and clouds, which means he's already begun entering the adult realm. If he falls completely out of the package now, he'll have to abort mission before ever even meeting Bina. He attempts to grab onto the inside of the blanket, but its smooth material is too slippery. His grip slides off of the gold, making a squeaking noise with his finger tips. Whoosh! He feels his body slide out following his head.

He closes his eyes, accelerating downward through the air, feeling the mist from the clouds dampen his newly formed skin. Just before he begins to sing the melody that will return him to his world and abort Bina's mission, "OUCH!" He yells out.

Scott dives down towards him. He pecks his gigantic iron-like beak at Cadence's body in order to rescue him, trying to grab him as gently as possible. First, Scott nips at his nose, then at his eyes and forehead. No success.

"Just use your claws to grab me, man! Why aren't you just using your clawed feet, which might I add are perfectly capable of a firm grip? Whhhyyyyy?" Cadence yells out in a panic.

Cadence realizes that his yelling at Scott isn't doing anything productive. So he decides to curl up in a ball, covering his face from the piercing chomps. This position reveals the back of Cadence's tender little head, which also gets nicked during the fiasco. Scott finally gets a firm clamp on Cadence's neck.

"Gotcha!" Scott mumbles holding onto Cadence's neck.

"Man this hurts! I'm definitely going to have some marks from this."

Cadence keeps his eyes shut to avoid further dizziness as Scott glides amid the clouds to the hospital where Bina awaits. Cadence feels himself plop down on an adult body. It's Bina! He then hears Scott say,

"We're here. Made it. Didn't miscarry you the whole way, so you're still able to complete your mission. No harm - no foul. Give me an excellent score on my deliverance tracker. Bye."

As fast as Scott says this, he's gone.

"That crazy rascal," Cadence repeats to himself, slightly disappointed at Scott's surprisingly poor performance today.

Cadence looks at Bina, as he sits on her chest. His vision is blurred because the universe doesn't grant permission for clear vision until the first few days of the assignment. This is so that each baby can pay attention to the connection with the adult, rather than the adult's external appearance. He feels the gold blanket drift down over him, and dissolve upon landing. Time is frozen for Bina.

He doesn't rush to turn her time back on because her countenance is so beautiful. He crawls up closer to her face. She smells so good, too. "You're more than a mission, Bina. I can tell we're gonna have lots of fun! I love you, so much already, and you don't even know it!"

Crawling back down across her belly and over her arm, he stretches out one tiny hand to tightly grip around her finger. He checks her heart beat through her finger, the way babies do when they calculate adult vital signs. The soft spot on the top of his head pulsates as its signal connects to the universe. He sings out in baby morse code, "raa – taa- taa – daa – daa -daa" for the universe to keep record of his findings regarding the introduction to the mission:

> Arrived safely to Assignment Bina. Had a couple hiccups along the way, causing me to create last minute melodies to place in Bina's memory to account for the time delay, as well as the 'battle scars' from the obstacles during the flight. (By the way, Pilot Stork Scott gets a score of 2 out of 10 for this delivery. I recommend he take

lessons on how to be more brilliant in his efficiency.) Bina matches her composition perfectly, and has received the connector program correctly. All responses are good. Everything is 'stimu' so far. Mission is viable and ready to commence. Bina and Mr. Bina now being admitted back into real time – adult world in 3-2-1.

Chord 4

Drones

Bina packs up her luggage while Cadence's father and grandmother bring the car to the front of the hospital. The doctor comes in as the nurse explains the discharge paperwork. The doctor advises Bina,

"It would be wise for us to do one final test before you take the little guy home. Just the standard check-out tests that I see we somehow overlooked. My apologies for the inconvenience."

"Well, what kind of tests?" Bina disconcertingly asks.

"Just a final weight check, temperature check, and a quick blood test."

Cadence smacks his lips and lets out a little grunt. Bina lovingly reassures him that everything is ok.

She reluctantly walks with the nurse to perform the tests in the room down the hall, anxious to get Cadence home already. Once they arrive to room 129, they take him from her arms to place him on the heated table.

"Weight: 6.5 pounds, very good little fella," the nurse remarks. "Next is temperature." She rolls a hand-held machine across his forehead, "Good! Now finally, a quick poke on the foot to draw some blood."

The nurse forcefully holds his foot in place and presses the needle into it. Blood spills out into the vile and onto the square napkin used to stop the trickling flow. Watching this hurts Bina more than Cadence. She tries to keep her cool so Cadence doesn't sense her nervousness. Inside, however, she feels everything from panic to rage to regret for allowing him to feel pain in any way, even if it is supposedly for his good.

Thankfully, though, he doesn't even flinch, let alone cry. He just keeps his eyes locked on her the whole time, like an obedient, trusting little boy. He's not worried because his mama is right there and would never let anything bad happen to him.

Bina squeezes his little hand, "I'm so proud of you son! Good job being so brave!"

He smiles back at her like he understands.

"Awe, you've got a smart baby, already responding to mama!" the nurse compliments Cadence's quick reaction.

Once Cadence and Bina arrive outside, their ride pulls up. Cadence's father opens the door for Bina, while the grandmother helps install Cadence's car seat. All the while Bina vents, "You guys just missed the saddest thing! Ugh... "

They buckle Cadence into the car seat and drive home, as Bina tells them about how well Cadence handled the last minute tests.

We see...

Finally, the mission may fully begin once Cadence is secured at the residence of Bina. Signs of departure to the home: Bina showered, dressed, and packing bags – check. Discharge papers – check!

"Wait a minute. What in the world is the doctor coming back in here for? Last minute tests? What the deuces is going on here?" Cadence thinks to himself. He smacks his lips and almost actually speaks to go off on the doctor for his staff's incompetency to complete all tests properly. He stops himself, and instead lets out a little grunt. He thinks, "Just let me go home with Bina already!"

The adults place him on the table, which feels cozy and warm. He doesn't mind that so much, especially since Bina is still right there next to him. But the minute Cadence sees the equipment, particularly the needle, in the nurses hand, he pauses time.

"Hold on, hold on, hold on! Crazy people want to do what? I'm outta here!"

He kicks the needle out of the nurse's hand. It freezes in mid-air preventing it from landing on the floor. He somersaults off the table, runs as fast as he can down the hallway, flailing his arms, and screams out, "Calling all drones, calling all drones." In an instant, an image of Cadence appears at the end of the hallway and says,

"We received your call for help. Drone 11 reporting for duty."

Cadence grabs his chest over his heart, and places one hand on the drone's shoulder. "Thank you for getting here so fast. You'd think that by now, I would be used to the whole hospital procedure. After hundreds of adult years doing it, ya know? But I keep forgetting what all is entailed in the modern tests, poking and probing of strange sorts. The adults who lived thousands of years ago weren't as complicated; I would simply arrive on the mission and get started."

The drone smiles, listening patiently with his arms folded, and agrees with Cadence by displaying a head nod.

"Your listening ear is much appreciated, old friend. But not as much as what you're about to do for me. Down the hall, room 129. Please call me when you're done."

The drone vanishes into thin air. After a second, Cadence hears a whistle from Room 129. He returns to the room, puts his hands on the door first, then cautiously peeks around the door into the room. He sees that the drone has completed the tests successfully.

"You may return to the table now, Cadence. I left off with Bina holding 'your' hand, saying how proud she is of 'you.'"

Cadence thanks Drone 11 again, and the drone disappears. Cadence climbs up onto the table and adjusts himself back into position. Time begins again, and he smiles up at Bina.

Bina interrupts the music in the travel bubble, "I remember that day like it was yesterday. Wait, so you never experienced any of that because the drone came in? What is a drone anyway?"

Cadence explains, "Drones are helpful entities that have the monotonous task of absorbing pain in order to destroy it. They mirror our physical appearance, then replace us for specified durations.

"They aren't from the same place we're from. But there are many of them. Drone 11, for instance, works with the medical division. Whenever anything requiring medical attention happens to babies in the adult world, Drone 11 and his division are called to step in. They have all kinds of drone sectors for different things to help us avoid pain in the adult world."

Cavatina chimes in, "We appreciate them very much because we need their help a lot in dealing with adults on earth. For some reason, the first adults on earth opted out of having access to drones because they thought adults *need* pain in order to feel joy. Very weird concept!"

Cadence continues, "Yes, very odd indeed! We babies intrinsically know that joy exists without any other conditions. Pain cannot exist without joy because pain's very essence is literally *the lack of joy*. But joy is in its own class;

it already existed before pain ever appeared. So joy doesn't need pain to exist."

He tells Bina that drones, therefore, cater to babies, to take their place in situations of pain, sickness or any other type of harm, including death. So babies don't actually feel the extent of any badness. And situations where drones are called upon are not pre-destined for any particular adult. Each mission is chosen at random by the universe, and never intended to teach some sort of "lesson" to adults, as many adults believe.

"Sometimes, drones even visit our world to help us. On occasion, the storks accidentally miscarry us to a wrong family or they miss a flight all together, preventing us from arriving at our assignment. We get pretty upset when they do this because it not only hurts our feelings that we couldn't complete a mission, but it must also devastate the adult expecting us or desiring that we one day arrive. It's a glitch in the system that we are working to fix. But in the meantime, the drones visit us on such occasions to prevent sadness from brewing, since our baby world can only sustain joy and curiosity. It cannot foster pain of any sort.

"In these circumstances, the universe takes over all details of the assignment from us, and supplies memories in the adult mind. So we have no idea of the final results for the adults or of their ultimate experience in those situations."

Cadence apologizes because he notices Bina's melancholy face from their candid explanation.

"It's ok!" Bina quickly replies. "I guess it's just a touchy subject in the adult world. Very emotional. But I'm glad you told me about this. It's great to know that drones are there so that babies don't have to deal with pain! We adults should NOT have ever opted out of having drones in the adult realm!"

Seeing that the mood needs some uplifting, Cadence says to Bina, "On a lighter note, remember when you accidentally hit my head on the doorway because you weren't yet used to carrying me around the house while multitasking? Well, guess what? That was a drone – wasn't me! I saw it coming from a mile away that you didn't estimate the distance accurately between my head and the wall, so I called the drones. Or that time you thought I rolled off the bed during the night and landed splat? Another drone, not me! Didn't feel a thing!"

Cavatina mentions a couple of the funny moments she got help from drones on assignment, too. They all share a laugh, making the feeling light-hearted again.

A yellow color suddenly makes a smooshing noise as it pours past the bubble. Cadence and Cavatina look at each other quickly,

"Poogon!" they yell out together like wild hyenas, throwing their hands in the air.

"Huh?!" Bina naively asks wanting to get in on the excitement.

"Just continue on with the memory you were just about to have," Cadence instructs her, "it's one of our favorite parts of the journey!"

Chord 5

All In The Details

Note-A, POOGON

B ina is super excited that Cadence has slept so well these first few nights at home. Tonight, as Cadence's father prepares for bed, Bina stays up wide awake rocking Cadence to sleep in the comfortable chair next to their bed and Cadence's bassinet. His eyes close so peacefully as he rests snuggled in her arms. She can't take his cuteness!

"I can stare at you and cuddle you forever and ever, Cadence!"

Her head feels like it's going to explode from how much she wants to squeeze him with so much love. She kisses him and kisses him and kisses him, taking in his fresh aroma. He smiles in his sleep with each kiss.

2 A.M. - Time to put him down so she can get some rest herself. Releasing Cadence from her arms is like pulling teeth from a dragonfish's tongue, nearly impossible. But she has to do it. She quietly scoots out of the chair and inches softly towards the bassinet. She slowly lowers him into the bassinet, protecting his head above all else. She removes her robe and slippers, and sits on the edge of the bed. "Nope, still too far away from me," she thinks to herself. She gently pulls the bassinet even closer to her side of the bed so that it actually touches the mattress. "Ok, that's better."

She lies down, covers herself with the blanket, and arches one arm over into the bassinet. This way, she can rest her hand on his chest to make sure he's still breathing through the night. She hears his breath and feels his tiny body pump air in and out. She hesitates to close her eyes because she doesn't want to miss a moment of his life. But she finally feels herself drifting into sleep.

2:20 A.M. - Bina jumps up at Cadence's cry. "Ok, ok, baby. It's ok." She picks him up and holds him to her chest. "Ssh, ssh, ssh."

Although she doesn't feel or smell anything, she reasons that he may need a diaper change. The room is dark, but she doesn't want to turn on the light to disrupt Cadence more or wake up his father. The night- light should be good enough she assumes.

She places him on her bed, opens his swaddled blanket, unhooks his onesie, and unlatches his diaper. With each action, she whispers "hi-ya" like she's in a karate tournament. She does this hoping it stops his cry while changing the diaper. And it works. He's quiet. She faintly sees his big eyes attempting to look up at her in the dark.

Before she can slide the clean diaper under him, a rapid explosion of poop bursts onto her hand and up her arm. It's hot and sticky, and smells a little like popcorn before it's too burnt to eat. She's in shock. What does she do? She is held hostage in the dark with one hand holding the baby in place, and the other now covered in excrement.

Someone sound the alarm, she needs help. "Honey, honey! Wake up and turn the light on, I need help!" she calls out to Cadence's father.

He instantly rises from his pillow, and turns on the ceiling fan by accident.

"No babe, the light – the light, not the fan!"

He scrambles to pull the cord for the ceiling light, after pulling the cord to the fan.

Cadence begins to cry again. Finally, light from the ceiling reveals the poopy massacre. Not only did Cadence shoot Dijon mustard looking poop onto Bina's hand and up her arm, but he managed to get some watery bits on Bina's pajamas, and all over her side of the bed. As well as on the side of the bassinet and on the floor. Cadence stops crying and wobbles his head slightly to look around at the debacle.

"What do I do now?" she humbly asks her husband, holding up her sticky poop covered limb.

He begins to laugh heartily, which makes her start to laugh as equally hard.

"Oh my goodness! This is crazy right?!" she belts out.

They laugh so hysterically that Bina starts coughing. Her husband rubs his tummy from aching ab muscles.

"Woo-wee! This boy and his shenanigans already. How did such a little guy do all this damage?"

"Well, he is *your* son, Bina," her husband says, wiping tears from his cheeks.

She rolls her eyes playfully at him. Glancing down at Cadence, who is smiling back at her, she says, "You're enjoying every minute of this, aren't you, my son?"

Cadence yawns and takes a deep breath.

"Whelp, let's clean this up, honey... somehow... I don't even know where to start."

We see...

Before she can slide the clean diaper under him, a rapid explosion of poop bursts onto her hand and up her arm. It's hot and sticky. Cadence gets up, moving at super speed so that Bina doesn't know, and follows the tracks into the bassinet.

"Poogon S-16! What an entrance! Well, I suppose *exit* fits more appropriately in this circumstance." Cadence enthusiastically approaches the small creature that resembles an amber-colored dragon, who sits at the head of the bassinet.

Its outer layer consists of thousands of transparent circular cells, overlapping like reptilian scales. The reddish gold color magnificently shines through from underneath the see-through scales, creating a lightning effect. It has four sets of wings trailing on each side of its body from the neck to the tip of the tail. These enable its super fast movement. Its stylish mohawk and naturally dark, sun-glass shaped eyes add a cool flare to the creature.

Cadence and Poogon S-16 slap hands then hug with one arm.

"Hey dude! Sorry about the scene. Your adult threw me off because she had no reason to change your diaper yet, so I wasn't expecting it. And then, with her repeatedly saying *hi-ya* with each action she did, I was busting up. It was hilarious! I couldn't stop laughing while waiting for my cue to exit. Was caught off guard by the time she got the diaper off. Had to kinda make an emergency break out of your diaper, ya know?"

"Of course, no worries! I know what you mean, Bina is quite the character. She's been cracking me up since I've been here. She barely sleeps because she'd rather stare at me. And don't even get me started on her conversations. Bruh-ther! Man, does she talk? She talks away, about whatever's on her mind. But she's goofy, that's what saves her from being irritating. The stuff that comes out of her mouth is a side-splitting riot!

"Anyhoo, man, look at the mess you just made! Your sulfur tracks are everywhere. Good thing for music speed, though, right? You got out just in time! I don't think the adults suspect a thing, though, because I've heard them say that they think the mess is digested milk leaving my body. Just the other day, Bina said that she thinks the tar exit road that you've been building in my diapers is digested fluid. That's loony how they think babies drink fluid that's produced by their bodies. They think milk just comes outta nowhere, and that we somehow live and grow off of that. I wonder if they've ever contemplated if *they* could survive off of just milk?"

Poogon S-16 replies, "I doubt it. Adults kinda just make up their own ideas and roll with them as fact, hardly ever looking back to verify the details. Let's face it, they've convinced themselves that it's logical. I guess it's just like how they've convinced themselves that babies should automatically have the same sleeping pattern that they do."

"I know, right?! How have they not figured out by now that we babies are nocturnal?"

They laugh together and shake their heads at the preposterous concepts.

"Ah, I love my baby life with these amusing adults."

Poogon S-16 opens his right claw to expose a piece of yellow cake, and says, "I love *my* life as a poogon. I get to eat tons of yellow cake uranium... Makes the diapers nice-n-*hot*!"

Cadence shakes his head and flares his nostrils in disgust, "How do you eat that stuff, mate?"

"What?! It's delicious! Don't judge, dude. You pretend to eat milk that supposedly comes from human bodies."

"Touche," Cadence yields to the Poogon's verbal jab.

"On a business note: The other poogons are scheduled to arrive accordingly over the course of your mission. Hopefully there won't be too many more explosions like this one I had to do today."

"Sounds great. I'm looking forward to them arriving."

They glance back at Poogon S-16's driblets of exploded debris.

"It will be entertaining to watch the adults figure out how to clean up the craziness you left behind! Feel free to plant the joy meters where you see fit. I'd recommend the kitchen and bathroom, as well as inside their vehicles. These adults seem to spend a lot of time in those places. I think the meters being there will easily monitor the balance of their joy, and utilization of it, when they're away from me."

"Thanks for the suggestion, Cadence. Sounds good. Enjoy your assignment, and I'll see you on the next mission."

"Thank you, Poogon S-16. As usual, I appreciate your assistance. See you again soon."

Bina interrupts the *you-see-we-see game* to ask about the surveillance meters.

Cadence explains, "The joy meters are designed to monitor the adult levels of joy under perplexing circumstances. Like lack of food, lack of sleep... "

Bina mumbles under her breath, "...Lack of the deed!"

Cadence and Cavatina look confusedly at Bina, then at each other.

"The deed?" They ask simultaneously.

"Ohhh, uhhh, never mind. I guess that's a part solely known by adults," Bina replies.

Cadence shrugs his shoulders in uncertainty, "Would you like to briefly explain 'the deed' please? I've heard you mention it before, but have never elaborated."

"It's not appropriate for a baby to hear the story of the 'deed.' Maybe if you were a teenager..."

Bina is cut off by sudden screeches from the babies grimacing faces.

"Yucky!" Cavatina blurts out, covering her ears.

"Please, Bina, don't compare us to those creatures of the teenage world or even imply that we will become them!" Cadence begs, with his hands pointed in prayer position. "They have the horrendous assignment of bringing distress and confusion, and yet are somehow happy in the misery of doing so. But that's another story for another day. It dampens our jolly moods. Just please don't mention them."

They both frown, and start to huff as their puppy-dog eyes fill with tears preparing for baby wailing. Out of motherly instinct, Bina automatically picks Cadence up into her arms, gently pushing his head down onto her chest. She also scoots Cavatina's little body close to her hip, and soothingly rubs her soft baby shoulder. In a quiet voice, she consoles them, "Ssshhh, ssshhh, ssshhh! Ok, ok, it's ok! I'm sorry for the interruption, and for the horrendous mention of *them*. Ok, so what happened after the poop dragon left?"

Cavatina rubs her eyes and nose, and gently pushes off of Bina's hip. Cadence lifts his head from her chest, looking up at her with blushed cheeks and pouting lips, and continues into the flashback:

Poogon S-16 scurries away in a flash, while Cadence trots back into position on the bed with Bina. He smiles up at her, holding in his laughter thinking about Poogon S-16's mess. Time resumes. Cadence gets a kick out of observing Bina's comical efforts to clean up the tracks of the Poogon.

After the commotion is over, and the adults finally fall fast asleep, Cadence records a little tune to the universe:

> Today, Poogon S-16 installed joy meters successfully. Test one complete. Adults found joy within a potentially joy-killing situation.

Note-B, MILK HIGH

Milk must be so yummy. Cadence's eyes roll back as he eats, like it's the best thing ever. He gulps quickly and slurps loudly, breathing hard, enjoying the feast. Bina runs her fingertips carefully over the silky soft strands of peach-fuzz on top of his head. In turn, he manages to reach one hand around to affectionately massage her back by folding his hand open then closed. She sighs, feeling calm and relaxed with every swallow he takes.

It satisfies her to know that not only are all of his nutritional needs being met, but also his emotional needs as well. Now that the treacherous and excruciating new feeding sensation has past, Bina looks forward to bonding with Cadence during feedings. These are the best moments for Bina. "Good nutrition will help you grow big and strong, bebe. So drink up."

His big, bright eyes creep up to look at her. He studies her with his mirror-like stare. He smiles, then returns to eating. His body feels warm from the heat generated between them. His eyes now drift down to look at Bina's armpit. He stares blankly. He no longer suckles, but instead babbles with his mouth full. Milk combined with drool leaks from the side of his mouth. His eyelids get heavy; they begin to close. She sits him upright to burp him, then scoots him back into a flat resting position snug in her arms.

He abruptly opens his eyes wide, fighting the sleep, and grunts loudly. His facial expressions go back and forth from smiling to frowning for no apparent reason. He oscillates back and forth from chuckling to whimpering. He drapes his forearm over his face. Then he runs his hand over Bina's mouth, and pats her collarbone area.

The nails on his other hand ironically scratch Bina's side, breaking skin. "Yikes, baby! Be careful!" she reprimands the sleepy boy. (No matter how much she cuts those nails, they grow with a vengeance!) He suddenly moves his arm from his face and throws it down to smack his own thigh a few times. Then pulls on his ear. His eyes get more and more droopy, until the babbling stops, and he finally falls asleep.

We see...

Joy molecules ready to reciprocate. What Bina believes to be feeding is actually an interchange of joy molecules between herself and Cadence. As she holds him close to her body, he is able to inject large amounts of joy directly into her bloodstream through his saliva and sweat, which enter through her pores. "Feeding" is the perfect diversion. He knows to latch on, inject, and un-latch.

He feels her relaxing as much as he is. Her breath is steady, her vibrations are calm, and everything feels good. He continues to rub her back, detecting her peace, while enjoying his head rub. Great! Task "feeding joy" accomplished.

But the more Bina relaxes him by massaging his head, the longer he stays latched on. He effortlessly returns the peace by massaging her back. He's so relaxed that he doesn't want to move.

Cadence suddenly feels a little too relaxed... light-headedness kicks in. He looks up at her with glossy eyes. His breathing becomes rapid, and he fights to keep his eyes open. He hits himself attempting to snap out of it. He recognizes he was accidentally latched on too long, and has accidentally ingested the fluid called "milk," too much too fast. He's drunk!

Speaking in very slurred baby morse code, he begins to ramble in a delusional condition:

"Don't, don't misconstrue my tory – my story. [eyes roll, and head falls forward slightly] My ambition is to gesticulate – [pause as if he forgot what he's talking about] ugh, uuummm – [burp!] - the nutritional value here is aggressive, it's so aggressive. I'm sorry, Bina. [whimpers, placing his arm over his face] Ssshhh, ssshhh, ssshhh my sweet. [puts his hand on her mouth] We've had some hard times, haven't we, old gurl? [clenches her collarbone, then loses muscle control and involuntarily hits her chest] You judge me, I judge you. We're in it together, though, that's not a lie."

In a high-pitched tone he continues,

"Pssssshhhh, milk doesn't come from your body. [condescendingly chuckles] It's a cow's job, Bina. It's a goat's job, Bina. It's a monkey's job, Bina. And so on and so forth. But not human am-ni-mals, for giving milk. THIS is what am-ni-mals do... " He scratches her side, breaking skin. He feels her jerk her side inward, and hears her say something to him.

"Oh no, I'm sorry!" [whimpers and slaps his thigh to snap himself out of it. He rubs his eye, then pulls on his ear] "I'm out of patrol – control. This is why we don't drink whatever comes from adult bodies. Cuz this is why it, what it... happens... if it happens." He knocks out.

Note-C. BOOGIE DOWN

"This little critter has completely stolen my heart," Bina proudly tells her friend over the phone about Cadence. Meanwhile, he reaches up trying to grab the cell phone from her ear. He keeps swinging his hands at the phone, but Bina pulls back and turns her head the opposite way so he can't reach. He tugs at her earring instead. She quickly turns her head again, "No, no, no baby. Don't do that. You'll hurt Mommy's ear." She gives him a peck on the forehead, and returns to her phone conversation.

"It's so stupid to think that I need to choose between working or spending quality time with my baby. It makes no sense to be forced to leave my baby just to return to a place I'm miserable at like 98% of the time. I'd rather be with Cadence, whereas 98% of the time I'm in absolute bliss. The 2% is frustration only from not having the power to prevent him from feeling bad and crying. Why does a mother have to choose between either losing herself to become what others need, or being herself and called selfish for it? Either way, it feels like we lose... with or without kids... the world makes us crazy. It's not the baby that makes it hard to be a mom! It's the world's set up that makes it hard to be a mom!"

Cadence persistently reaches for the phone again. She repeats the same aversion movements. He tugs at her shirt this time, rather than her earring. She pulls her shirt up with the same hand she holds the phone in. He brutally knocks the phone out of her hand onto the hard floor. "Cadence! Calm down! Peanut, are you hungry?"

After hanging up with her friend, she attempts to feed him, but he refuses to eat. "You just wanted me off the phone, and all to yourself, I guess."

He smiles and claps his hands together.

She hands him a toy, and he shoves it in his mouth. They play for a while, then she selects a book to read to him. He shoves the pages of the book in his mouth half way through the story. She removes the paper from between his gums, and he takes the opportunity to chew on her finger.

"You're so silly, putting everything in your mouth these days. You must be relieving the pain of your incoming teeth. C'mon, let's get you something cool to chew on."

As she walks to the refrigerator, the radio plays "Come Together," by The Beatles. Cadence pumps his chest to the beat. She notices his rhythm, and begins to pop her shoulders in sync with his movements. She sways her hips. He puts both arms in the air and waves them to the beat. She propels him into the air just above her head, then whirls around in the middle of the kitchen. He's so serious about the music it makes Bina laugh.

Time flies by as different songs play. Bina jumps around to the Red Hot Chilli Peppers, "Snow (Hey Oh)" singing the lyrics loudly. "I love these lyrics! If you wanna know how mama feels the majority of time when it comes to dealing with the world, listen to these lyrics, cuz' they'll tell ya."

Cadence responds to her excitement by mimicking her singing, yelling out along with the tune, and bouncing in her arms.

The music changes to "Love Is My Religion" by Ziggy Marley. "Yay!!!" She grabs one of his little hands and waves it in the air. "Remember the words to this song, always, my son."

He bobs his head to the beat. She tickles his exposed armpit, and he laughs sincerely from the gut, causing his body to tense.

When Beethoven's "Fur Elise" starts to play, they begin to slow dance. Cadence now rests his head on Bina's shoulder. She forgot why they walked into the kitchen in the first place.

"That was quite a show," Cadence's dad surprises them as he walks into the room.

"Were you there the whole time?" she asks.

"Just half-way into the Ziggy song. Cadence sure is going to like a wide range of music. You play him everything under the sun."

"Of-course," she scoffs, "He needs to be well-rounded. Plus, he responds better to music than anything else I do with him."

Cadence leans over for his dad to embrace him.

Bina hands Cadence over. "So, my mom is coming over to spend the night. Which is great because I'm so exhausted and need a little break."

"A break? A break from what?"

Bina glares at him. "Are you serious, dude? Are you seriously asking me why I need a break? You should be asking me how I'm still going with all that I do."

"Ok, ok. Simmer down. I didn't mean to ruffle your feathers. How about I take Cadence for a couple hours tomorrow after your mom leaves so you can have some time to yourself?"

"Well, ok... although it's not really *Cadence* I need the break from," she sarcastically replies.

"Oooo, burn! You're so mean, Bina," he wisecracks back at her. "I'm off to work now. I'll see you guys later." He hands Cadence back to Bina after giving him multiple kisses on his cheeks.

We see...

"This little critter has completely stolen my heart," Bina proudly tells her friend over the phone about Cadence. Meanwhile, he reaches up trying to grab the cell phone from her ear. He keeps swinging his hands at the phone, but Bina pulls back and turns her head the opposite way so he can't reach.

The technological waves from the phone interfere with Cadence's clear connection to the universe. His ears ring with disruption. He can't take it anymore. He thinks to himself,

"I need to get that dreadful thing away from us. If it's doing this to *my* mind, it MUST be messing up Bina's, too. She doesn't seem to acknowledge any discomfort from it, though, because she's been talking for over an hour and still going. Sometimes technology gets more attention than I do!"

He finally comes up with a plan. If he can create a distraction, making her think he's trying to grab something else that he's not supposed to have, he can speedily snatch the phone away. He tugs at her earring. She quickly turns her head again, "No, no, no baby. Don't do that. You'll hurt Mommy's ear." She gives him a peck on the forehead, and returns to her conversation.

"Drats! That didn't work," he thinks.

He reasons that he'll try the straight forward attack one last time. He persistently reaches for the phone again. She repeats the same aversion movements.

"She's good. But I will not be defeated. I'm doing this for your own good, Bina. Just trust me."

He tugs at her shirt this time, rather than her earring, knowing that she cannot avert from that. Just as he planned: she pulls her shirt up with the same hand she holds the phone in. Without warning, he brutally knocks the phone out of her hand onto the hard floor. She finally gets the hint, and hangs up. Instantly, the ear-piercing interference stops.

Now he needs to make sure that his surroundings are still safe. He follows the appropriate baby protocol of tasting everything in order to document whether the immediate environment is familiar and secure. After tasting a reasonable amount of items, he confirms that the coast is clear. Per usual, he nibbles on Bina's finger to let her know he's done with his taste tests, and ready for a change of scenery.

As Bina carries him to the fridge, he hears a catchy song. He's captured by the beat, and the words that complement it perfectly. He feels compelled to groove once he hears the lyrics: *One thing I can tell you is you got to be free.* He observes Bina letting loose, too, swaying her hips to the music.

They bask in the ambience of the music. Cadence hasn't stopped time as they dance, but it feels as though he has. They're in their own little world together, moving in vibrational harmony with the universe through dance. The joy they project is so powerful that it enlightens the bad moods of hundreds of sad moms somewhere around the world.

He lifts his head up from her shoulder. He begins to utter the first word she will hear him say, but is cut-off by Mr. Bina entering the room. Now is not the time to tell Bina, but soon. The next time she feels free and in complete peace, he will tell her she's the chosen one.

Cadence listens to their brief conversation, disturbed at Mr. Bina's poor choice of wit. "You joke of Bina's hard work, do you, Mr. Bina? You're a cool mate, but you sure don't know how to charm the ladies. How did Bina ever fall for *you*? Yes, take me out tomorrow! Let's just see how easy it will be for you when I scream uncontrollably, vomit all over your new shirt, and kick the glasses off of your face as you change my diaper. Maybe you'll have a little more appreciation for Bina, after our little play-date tomorrow."

Note-D. PEE-CULIAR BEHAVIOR

Bina's jaws clench at her mother's remarks. The visit started out well, with lots of hugs, love, and kisses for both Bina and Cadence. Bina was able to give her tired body a rest from constantly holding Cadence, as well as dish out all the cool updates on Cadence's development. Not to mention, eat up all the yummy home-cooked food brought over. But as the evening progresses, Cadence's grandmother makes sure to give Bina her two cents on parenting... make that 10 cents, of what is starting to sound like *non-sense* in Bina's head.

She critiques everything Bina is doing or plans to do with Cadence, without truly listening to Bina's input.

"So, I notice he's so tense. Do you stretch him every day? And he's not the average size that most babies are. Are you feeding him right? Maybe he needs more activity, or maybe more rest. Are you swaddling him tight at night? And please don't tell me you're letting him fall asleep in your arms during naps and before bedtime! You've got to put him down as soon as he begins falling asleep or he's going to get used to you always being there for him..."

"... But isn't that the point of a mother: making sure your child feels safe, and knows you will be there whenever you're able..."

"Bina- baby, I'm your mother. I know what I'm talking about. But hey, if you want him to be spoiled rotten, depending on you for every little thing in life, you'll keep doing what you're doing. It's none of my business. One more thing: do you make time to talk to him and read to him constantly?"

"I actually sing to him more than anything because he seems to like it."

"Oh no, baby. You've got to read more than anything. That's the only way to really fine-tune his development. Oh, and one of my doctor friends told me to make sure he gets all his shots. They didn't have the amount of shots when you were a baby, or even when I was young. So you need to make sure to take full advantage of all the preventative care available. Do everything that they tell you to do. What's-her-name is always posting pictures online of herself reading to her baby, and saying how she has her baby up on all of her baby's shots. That could be why her baby is growing differently and performing differently than Cadence..."

Bina walks to the couch so her mom can't see her infuriated face. Her nostrils flare like a raging bull, and she rolls her eyes for only Cadence to see. Although reluctant to speak up for herself, she cannot contain the furnace inside that's about to blow.

"Ok, Mom. Let me stop you right there," tilting her head towards her shoulder, stretching her neck.

Cadence wraps his hand around her finger. He softly pinches the skin on her arm, as if trying to stop her. He raises his eyebrows at Bina. Then quickly swivels his head in the direction of his grandma, and waves at her.

Bina swallows hard. "No disrespect, because I appreciate your concern for us, and willingness to offer your experience. But do not *ever* compare my baby to someone else's, ok. I am NOT one of those insecure parents who competes with every other mom about what size, shape or color Cadence is. I don't care what other parents are doing because I'm focused on what *I'm* doing! And I don't care what Cadence is doing in comparison to other babies! He's lovable, affectionate, highly responsive, has a good measure of health, and most of all, is <u>happy</u>. Those all blend together to make him the perfect amount of beautiful and intelligent.

"You know what else? It's so sad that innocent babies are forced into the crossfire of ignorant, judgmental, jealous adults. Babies only want to give and receive joy. Honestly, we should learn from them, instead of inadvertently teaching them how to become self-absorbed jerks!

"Plus, all people are individuals, right?! No better, no worse, just different. Therefore, different isn't bad, it's normal. It's the essence of what being human is. That goes for babies, too, Mom.

"And on a side note: babies are NOT trained monkeys *performing* their daily actions for our entertainment. Yea it's cool to capture some pictures of them growing at their own pace, and a few funny little moments. But for goodness' sake: Can people paa-lease just enjoy their children without egotistical competitions with or prejudices against other little ones?! Any adult who lives in constant competition about babies, needs to grow up, get a life, and learn to *really* love themselves and the babies they claim to cherish!"

She vents to her mom all the words that she actually wants to say to so many other people every single day but doesn't. Her heart thumps through her shirt, and she feels the blood rushing through her veins, making her shaky.

Cadence looks disconcertingly at Bina. His face frowns like he wants to cry. Bina notices his dismay, and takes a deep breath. She needs to rectify her imploding anger before Cadence senses it and mistakenly thinks he caused it. She walks into the kitchen where her mom silently stands, shocked by Bina's words.

Bina adjusts the mode of the conversation, since her intention isn't to make her mom feel bad. "But enough of that! You know what I desperately need your help with, Mom? Bath-time! Do you mind giving Cadence a bath please, while I take my own to relieve some stress?"

"Of course, baby," she replies lovingly. "And Bina, I apologize if I offended you or came across as scolding. I'm very proud of you! You're an industrious, patient wife, and an incredibly attentive mother. Your instinct to protect and confidently defend your son is very inspiring. I know that because of your intense love for Cadence, he will become a respectable, strong, honest man."

Bina and her mother embrace tightly, with Cadence caught in the middle. He lets out a little grunt. She, and Bina, separate and laugh at his funny facial expression, as he fluctuates his look from Bina, to his grandmother, and back to Bina again.

"Go get yourself in that bath. Light some candles, put some music on. Do what you've got to do. I'll take care of Cadence's bath."

We see...

Cadence wonders how the tempo changed so quickly, from everyone feeling joyful, to Bina's mother offering up unwarranted critiques, and Bina getting hot like a sauna. "Poor, Bina," he thinks to himself. "She's getting bombarded with negative energy about things that are so small. And I'm a tiny baby, so if I say something is small, you know it's small. Wait a minute, I remember Cavatina telling me all about this adult's mothering skills – she has no room to give Bina any criticism!"

He watches Bina become increasingly upset as her mother babbles on and on, talking about nothing. He sees Bina roll her eyes. Then he suddenly hears a pop as she stretches her neck, tilting her head to the side.

"Ooooo, Lady! You'd better run. Bina is about to blow. Her vitals are off the charts. I'll try to hold her back."

He removes his hand from Bina's finger, and pinches her arm, but to no avail. She doesn't even notice. "Whelp, I can't stop her." He swivels his head in the direction of Bina's mom, "You're on your own now." Waving at her, he hopes that she'll heed his warning and take cover. But she tenaciously stands there.

Despite his initial fear of Bina becoming overly emotional, he is now actually very proud of her. He listens as she articulates what he knows she has been holding in for so long. He feels vindicated and safe, knowing that Bina has his back no matter what. And not just his back, but that of all babies... which technically is still mostly his back, when it's not Cavatina's. He thinks it's *stimu* that she displays such bold moxie, yet in a respectful and tactful way.

"Well said, Bina!" he thinks to himself. "Yea, let's wash up. I got a little gift during bath-time for you, *Graaand-Maaa*."

Bina walks out of the room and disappears around the corner. The older adult prepares the bath water in his plastic mini-tub, and picks up the yellow plastic baseball bat that he plays with during bath-time. She places him slowly into the bath water, and hands him the toy bat. She begins washing his body. She slathers him in soap suds from his ears, to his neck, back and tummy.

"You have a lot of ear wax. Your mama hasn't been paying close enough attention to your little ears, has she?"

He thinks, "What'd you say about my mama?! Of course there's plenty of ear wax in my ears. That's how babies filter the badness that adults like to spew out. No matter how much cleaning any adult does, the ear wax will always be there. You got a problem with the design, talk to the universe about it!"

"You're just a little talker, aren't you, baby?" She says in response to his baby morse code.

She moves on to scrubbing his arms and hands. In an annoying baby voice, she says, "Otay, gib gwamma da bat pweez. I can't wash your hands if you're holding the toy."

He holds on tightly, looking at her without an expression. They struggle for a second playing tug-of-war with the toy. He thinks, "Yes, move a little closer in... closer... closer."

"Let grandma see the bat, bebe." She leans in closer to him attempting to unlatch his grip.

He hangs on relentlessly, waiting for the perfect moment to...

She screams and steps back away from Cadence immediately. Pee streams out at her like a fountain. It's flying out everywhere, spraying onto her clothes, all over the counter and floor. Some even sprinkles her face.

"And that's what else the universe has programmed in us: we mark our territory from potential predators. Bina is mine. Nobody hurts her feelings and gets away with it!"

The pee finally stops. Cadence laughs.

"Oh wow, baby boy. You sure do have some power there. Gotta be careful with that."

As she bends down to clean up the floor, Cadence catches sight of Bina peeking from around the corner at them. She has her hands over her mouth, covering her laughter. That's the funny Bina he likes to see. He flashes a huge grin at her and pounds on the water, splashing to create more mess for his grandma. Bina accidentally lets out a snort through her fingers, then quickly covers her nose as if that will take back the sound.

Bina's mother looks up to find Bina highly amused. "Alright. I guess I forgot what hidden treasures can happen at bath time."

"Uh hunh," Bina replies with a valiant smile that silently declares *Yep, NOBODY is the perfect mom because babies do what they want, when they want, how they want.*

"How about you go change your clothes, Mom. I have a couple minutes before my tub finishes filling up. I'll stay here with him til' you get back to finish his bath."

After the grandmother walks out, Cadence and Bina look at each other.

"You got her for me, didn't you, my little man?"

"Yes, yes I did, my Bina," he replies in baby morse code.

He notices her face doesn't look as happy as it normally does.

She smiles, but her eyes are puffy and slightly red. He sees that her cheeks are damp from tear tracks. His heart tingles with a funny feeling, similar to the one he begins to feel right before the drones need to be called. But instead of calling on the drones, he lets himself feel whatever feeling is starting to happen.

He needs to know why he feels like this. He's curious to understand why Bina's face looks so sad. He stops time to sing out a special request to the universe. He asks for permission to review the footage from Poogon S-16's joy monitor in Bina's bathroom. "I'd like to see what Bina saw that made her cry unhappy tears, please."

He hops down off the counter, and shuffles into the bathroom. He climbs up onto the sink and stands in front of the mirror. "Where is that re-play switch?" He presses both hands against the mirror and taps it in various spots. He also presses his mouth on the mirror, licking it, leaving steamy breath and saliva on it.

During his search, he makes eye-contact with himself. He realizes it's the first time he has seen his image since starting Bina's missions. "So this is what Bina envisions me to look like? Not too shabby! One of the best looking babies I've ever morphed into for sure."

He flexes his little biceps. Then he rotates around to check out his body from behind in the mirror. "Oh wow, another birthmark smack-dab on my bottom. Scott really needs to stop FWT – Flying While Tired!"

He turns back around to face the mirror, and rubs his tummy. "Plump, round tummy. That's what I'm talking about. Nothing more cute than a baby's chunky tummy." He smiles at himself.

Remembering that he needs to find the re-play button on the poogon's joy monitor, he leans his whole body against the mirror. Continuing to search, he raises a foot against the mirror, and !Click!. A song begins to play. A sad song. He steps back and watches the monitor through the mirror.

The joy meter flashes a red alert: *Insufficient Joy, Level E (empty)*. An image of Bina looking at herself in the mirror appears. She touches her hair, then her face, then her stomach, and cries. However, the image Bina sees of herself is totally false.

Cadence sees a reflection of a monster standing in front of Bina. Discolored skin, dark under-eye circles, and deep scars cover the monsters whole body. These ugly marks particularly show on the chest, abdomen and thigh areas. The monster's frumpy proportions are unrealistically out-of-shape. Hair sheds from its head in chunks, creating massive bald spots. Its eyes are dull, as if the life has been sucked out of them. He doesn't understand why Bina thinks this monster is herself.

As the monster stands there, crying and moaning, a slew of negative words create the lyrics to the sad melody:

Unattractive
Out-of-shape
Un-wanted
Sleep-deprived
Over-worked
Anxious
Inexperienced
Unworthy
Misunderstood
Under-appreciated
Misguided
Selfish
Should... be... happier.

This causes Cadence to cry. Not the programmed cry meant to test the adults' patience and endurance. But a cry from deep within his being... a cry from a broken heart. He's never felt this before.

"Bina, none of that it true! That's not you," he speaks out loud, although the re-played image cannot hear him. "You're the most beautiful mother ever! You nurture life and joy, so it's impossible that you could be anything *but* beautiful.

"And why do you feel unwanted? *I* want you. Mr. Bina wants you. Yeah, he sometimes takes you for granted, not acknowledging all the many things that you do, and do quite well. But he works very hard as your partner in this baby mission because he loves you very much. When you're not looking, he stares at you like you're his favorite person in the world – even more than me.

"Sure, other people are obnoxious with their little comments, and sometimes overbearing with their critiques and advice. But another person's opinion isn't the final truth. And *their* inability to be happy for us, Bina, doesn't mean you are flawed in all these ways you think you are. Neither am I flawed simply because *they* think I am."

He questions whether it was a wise choice to allow himself to feel these feelings.

"Am I not doing a good enough job as a baby, bringing you a positive distraction in an unhappy world? What's my purpose if I'm not bringing joy into Bina's world?"

Once he starts questioning his purpose, he snaps himself out of the danger of discouragement. Recognizing that he's thinking more like an adult instead of a baby, by doubting his life's purpose, he forces his thoughts back towards joy. After all, adults ask and doubt because they learn from external factors how to strengthen themselves – from the outside in. Whereas babies learn from internally knowing to *just be*, from the inside out.

"Bina, prepare for the best cheering up you've ever had in your life! Time to turn up the charm, Cadence, to remind her of the joy she deserves."

Note-E. KISSING MAGNETS

"Sun Is Shining" by Bob Marley wakes Bina up on her alarm the next morning. She decides to let the whole song play. She turns over to Cadence, who is already wide awake, smiling, waiting for her to turn attention to him. "Well, good morning, Peanut. How's my little fella doing this morning?"

He stares deeply into her eyes. There's something about this little guy that makes her feel like she's the only person in the world who matters. She loves the feeling that only he can give her. He lifts his hands to caress her cheeks. Her hair cascades over him, surrounding him like a waterfall. He gently strokes the messy strands that engulf him. She kisses his nose, then his neck. He lets out a robust laugh.

Cadence keeps laughing out loud for no reason. His lips are rounded and wide open, revealing the inside of his mouth. His tongue curls up on both sides while the middle sticks to the bottom. It vibrates rapidly as he laughs, "Aaahhh yaaa haaa haaa haaa!"

Automatically, Bina laughs at his laughter. He analyzes her laugh with animated eyes. He screams out another goofy laugh, making Bina laugh more. They laugh together for a minute.

He pets her hair again. She sees how completely enamored he is by her. His eyes follow her closely with every movement. She can't help but to kiss his alluringly soft skin. "Can I kiss you forever and ever, until forever ends, Son?"

The song switches to Lenny Kravitz, "I belong to you." She sings along, serenading Cadence. He laughs, and pulls her head down to his face by her hair so that she can kiss him again. She gladly obliges, and gives him a big kiss on his cheek. "Yummy yummy kisses!"

She almost can't stop kissing him. He receives her show of affection with vulnerable acceptance and appreciation. He puckers his lips to return the love. When she pulls up from kissing him, he says, "Mum-mum-mum-mum."

"Cadence! Are you saying yum-yum, like yummy kisses? Or are you saying mum mum, like mom mom? Either way, you're so smart! I love you so much! You kick my love into overdrive. When I'm with you I feel so happy. It's like, all my other thoughts just disappear, and I feel important and meaningful. Thank you for giving me the gift to smile another day!"

We see...

Cadence lies awake in the bed after hearing Mr. Bina leave for work. He knows that Bina's alarm will go off soon, and he eagerly waits for her to open her eyes. Once she turns her attention to him, he releases magnetic compounds through his skin, making it soft and irresistibly kissable. The magnets pull out Bina's joy with each kiss, until she oozes with happiness.

Cadence interrupts the memory in the travel bubble, "As far as everything else, Bina, that wasn't a programmed part of the mission. I truly laughed with you because I like to see your smile. I pet your hair because it's lovely, no matter what style it's in (or not in). And I stare at you from my heart, not with my eyes, because I truly adore you." He smiles up at her with sparkling eyes, and they embrace.

"Awe!" Cavatina remarks.

Chord 6

Beyond The Mission

Bina feels the travel bubble drifting downwards, and notices that it is beginning to stretch out of shape. "What's happening?"

"We don't have much time left. Your memories have stopped because your mind is more clear and your heart is overflowing with the stillness of peace."

Cavatina explains some of the short gaps that were left unanswered during the journey in the travel bubble thus far.

She begins with how babies exchange information through vomit. She recounts a funny story about how she vomited in Cadence's face because she was so excited to share the information of her mission with him, that when she saw him, she let it rip. "All the information that adults vocalize with words, is contained in our vomit."

Bina makes a grossed-out face.

"Might seem sick to you, but it's normal to Cadence and me." She and Cadence nod their heads together in agreement. "We don't even need to be directly around each other's vomit to retrieve the information from it either."

She proceeds to explain the reason why babies have such a short assignment. "The universe restricts prolonged exposure to adults. We aren't allowed to stay with adults too long because if we do, we'll become tainted, and begin losing our pure innocence. Once we begin to exhibit adult attributes, the universe ends our assignment.

"For instance, signs that we are becoming more adult-like are when we begin morphing beyond babyhood. Like growing teeth, looking more defined or specifically like one adult or the other, soft spots closing up, and so on."

Cadence interjects, "As you've already learned, our soft spots are our direct link to the universe. It's like recharging our battery, which is why it pulsates. Connectors go in and out constantly like lightning. Imagine lightning bolts blasting in and out of your brain non-stop. That's pretty much what our soft spots do. And the thing we're recharged with is purity, goodness and joy. Basically, we're filled with the music of the universe through our soft spots."

"So when they begin to close," Cavatina finishes the thought, "We begin to lose this direct link to music, and begin to lose our innocence."

"... Because losing innocence and developing hard heads means becoming more adult-like?" Bina asks.

"Exactly," Cavatina confirms. She adds, "That's why we babies have the shortest assignment with adults. But even though we have the shortest duration with you guys, we make the most long-term impacts. We determine the hard-wiring that the kid realm will set for personality, looks and thinking ability. We set everything up for them to complete their assignments according to their missions. We provide the essentials that adults need to experience pure, unadulterated happiness."

"So, are you guys sent to us to deliver joy? Is that your mission?"

"Our mission is to be delivered. We don't have joy, we **are** joy. Babies are joy personified. We are sent to share ourselves. And by our sharing joy, adults are protected."

"Protected from what?"

"From losing hope that good things do exist among you. Joy is the foundation of endurance; and hope, the foundation for joy. Simply put, we give you the boost to smile another day," Cadence answers.

Bina responds, "What you're saying makes perfect sense. Babies do give so much joy by simply existing. Whether an adult is a parent or not, a cute and lovable little baby creates joy in their heart. I guess it's not the big things in life but the little ones that matter most."

"And that's why I chose you, Bina. There's a point when certain adults, like yourself, begin to realize the 7th sense. It's the strongest sense: the ability to see the world as a baby does, through the eyes of pure joy. To let go of all inhibitions and just live. Now you have come to know babyhood – joy."

"I'm so honored. Thank you."

They share a moment of loving silence.

"But, to be honest," Bina continues, "I feel like there are still things left unanswered."

"Because there are. If we were to explain every single thing that babies see, learn, experience, and provide to adults, the journey would never end. That's why we allow your memories to guide our explanation. To explain the parts of babyhood that have been most special to you."

"Oh. Ok. Well, real quick, what about things like: all those times your eyes twinkled when you smiled at me during play time? Or when you would stare into my eyes and caress my face or my hair? Or when you would clap and laugh whenever I'd walk into the room? What did things like that mean?"

Cadence answers, "That all meant that I love you."

Bina pauses. She feels a knot in her throat. She tries to fight the tears. But they escape from her eyes with a vengeance. She knows the trip is coming to an end. Cadence gestures for her to pick him up.

She lifts him up into her arms and embraces him tightly. She squeezes her eyes shut as they burn with tears, like volcanoes erupting.

"I will always love you, Bina. You're my favorite adult."

Still holding him tight, she replies, "I will always love you, my son." She kisses his ear.

She can't bring herself to let go of the embrace in order to look at his face. With a sniffle, she asks, "What now? Will I ever see you again?"

"No, you won't because your baby journey has passed. You'll move on to the kid stage now. I'll send my report of your composition to the kid world. Don't worry, I'll make sure that your kid- Cadence will treat you well. Although you won't consciously remember all the details of this tour, you'll always remember the important parts when your joy meter is low. And you'll never forget the love you feel for your baby. This love will be the strongest love of all your journeys. So strong, that it will bond you to all the realms beyond this baby mission.

"When we release from this embrace, your travel bubble will burst. You will automatically advance into the next stage of your personal journey. Take all the joy that we have shared with you forever and ever, until forever ends."

"I will. Thank you for the *stimu* experience. You've made me so happy. I'll miss you so much! I'll treasure the memories of waking up to your smiling face, and hearing your exaggerated yawns when you're sleepy, and holding you snugly-wugly, and endlessly kissing your chubby cheeks. I think most of all, I'll miss staring into your vivacious eyes."

"I'll arrange for the kid- Cadence to have my eyes, then."

"Thank you," Bina chuckles at his never ending desire to bring her joy. "I love you more than you'll ever know, Cadence!"

"I love you more!"

"Cadence, my heart hurts to think that I can't go back! I don't want my baby to be gone... "

****

Bina opens her eyes. Her five year old son gazes adorably at her with his big sparkling eyes.

"Nuh-unh, that's not really how I got here mom. Storks can't carry babies. They're too heavy."

She's totally thrown off. She has no idea what he's talking about. Actually, it feels like she's never even seen him before, yet she *knows* this is her son. Her head aches as if she has been crying really hard and really long. But obviously, she hasn't been.

Rubbing her head, partly from pain and partly from confusion, she asks, "What, Cadence? What was I telling you? Of course storks don't carry babies, silly."

"But that's what you just said. Why did you say that then?"

"I don't know. Mama is goofy sometimes. I just like to see if you'll believe me, I guess."

She raises his arm and tickles his underarm. He squirms and giggles uncontrollably, compressing his arm into his side with all his strength, hoping it will prevent her from continuing the task.

"The tickle monster, the tickle monster! She's getting you but you cannot break free from her power!"

He laughs, and grabs her hand with his other hand. "Oh yes I can! I can beat up the tickle monster! Hi-ya!" He does a soft karate chop to her arm.

"Ah, ok ok. You win."

"Mom, you said I'm from another planet. Was that a joke, too?"

Bina doesn't remember saying any of this. She replies, "I said that, too, did I? That one might be true. You are a little alien if I've ever seen one."

"Hey!" he karate chops her collarbone area.

"Peanut, play nice. You gotta be gentle with the ladies, babe! It's not so bad to be an alien resident. Just means you're different from the natives in a certain land, and that you'll stay temporarily. Which is true, because we all grow up. So we're all temporarily in one stage of our lives, then we move on to the next. We're all temporary aliens in this life. But I have to admit: you're the most wonderful, most important and the cutest little alien I've ever had in my life!"

She tickles him again. He laughs out, "Nooo, I can't breathe!!!"

A splash in the background interrupts their tickling festivities. They both look to see a large stork floating on the lake, lightly splashing himself.

"Scott..." Bina says in an undertone.

"What'd'you say, Mommy?"

"I said 'Scott.' I dunno why. For some reason, that bird looks like its name would be Scott. Don't you think?"

"Eh, kinda. I guess. If animals have names," Cadence answers in an uninterested tone.

They watch the bird together in silence before it finally flies away.

"Let's go inside now, babe. I have a major headache, and need a nice tall glass of water."

They hold hands, and walk past the lake, and down the trail that leads to their house. Skipping energetically, he asks, "Why did you name me Cadence?"

"Because you're the beat in my heart and the music of my life."

****

"And that's one of the examples that explain the baby mission, which is to bring joy to the adults," states the Baby Professor standing in front of the class full of kids ranging from ages 2 to 9 years. They all pay close attention to the professor's lecture.

He continues to instruct, "The baby mission is joy in all capacities. There was an ancient time when no babies existed among adults on earth. There was no joy. So the universe called us to bring that joy to them. Our presence gave them a sense of power and confidence in their adult race. They concocted the idea that they pro-created us. So, we rolled with it, focused on the mission."

The kids astutely jot down notes.

"And this is where you kids enter the picture. Once our mission is complete, you take over the assignment. Your commission is to teach patience and make the adults use their imaginations. The adolescent realm is to teach forgiveness and fortitude. Their commission is to mirror the most negative aspects of the adults they are assigned to. You will communicate with the adolescent realm once your assignments are complete. But we'll get into the details throughout this semester's course."

Unanimously, the older kids burst out in excitement at the prospect of networking with adolescents, "Cool!"

"Simmer down, class. Are there any questions?"

Nobody raises their hand.

"If not, we'll resume class tomorrow 9 AM sharp. Please be prepared for a brief exam on what we covered today. Class dismissed."

Two of the older kids sitting in the top row of the classroom, Leilani and Brad, gather their notes from their desks and push them into their backpacks.

Brad asks Leilani, "Isn't it crazy to think that there actually exists an earth full of adults? All this time, I thought that only we and the adolescent realm lived on the earths in the universe."

"Yea, it's crazy!" Leilani answers. "But it's even crazier that we have to work with the adolescent realm. Although they're kinda cool, they're also a little scary. Don't you think?"

Brad puffs his little chest out, "Nah! We'll be alright. They can't be any scarier than we kids can be at three years old!"

They walk down the hall together towards the library to study for tomorrow's exam.

To Be Continued ...

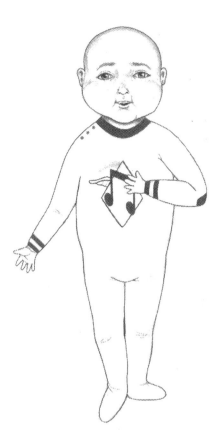

The lovable, kissable, and irresistibly stinky
CADENCE

Rock On! You little cutie-pie, CAVATINA

SCOTT. *Enough said.*

Kewl, dude! POOGON S-16

Post-pardum Mirror Monster Bina.

About the Author

Amber Owens is an unconventional fiction author, writing to inspire other beautiful minds. She holds a Bachelor's Degree in English, Writing and Literature. Amber's creative work is intended to spark the imaginations of all ages. She lives with her family in Southern California.

Printed in the United States
By Bookmasters